Esperanza

SPIRIT
of the CIMARRON

Esperanza

by KATHLEEN DUEY

DREAMWORKS

TM & © 2002 DreamWorks LLC
Text by Kathleen Duey
All rights reserved.

Published in the United States 2002 by Dutton Children's Books,
a division of Penguin Putnam Books for Young Readers
345 Hudson Street, New York, New York 10014
www.penguinputnam.com
Printed in USA First Edition
ISBN: 0-525-46859-5

1 3 5 7 9 10 8 6 4 2

The characters and story in this book were inspired by the
DreamWorks film *Spirit: Stallion of the Cimarron*.

Chapter One

The second winter of my life was gray and cold and long. The willow stands in our sheltered mountain valley were grazed flat. Our lead mare and our stallion died of hunger. So did many of the others. We were all weakened. My mother, Alma, was both shy and small—like me. But she was also stubborn and brave. She decided we had to leave before the snow melted—or starve. Most of the herd stayed behind, too weak or too afraid to travel while the ground was still snow-covered. It was a terrible time. The herd I had been born into scattered like cottonwood seeds in the wind.

Esperanza placed her hooves carefully, following her mother down the steep, muddy path. Alma had been going slowly and she hesitated often on the icy trail. Esperanza glanced back. Three other mares were strung out behind her, walking single file close to the canyon's edge.

The days had warmed just enough to begin melting the snow. Far below, at the bottom of the canyon, the river ran hard and fast. There was white foam swirling around the boulders that jutted above the dark water.

The little band of mares left deep prints in the thawing mud. Esperanza stayed close to her mother. Alma insisted on plodding along, and Esperanza had little choice but to walk slowly and deliberately.

Esperanza knew it was safest to move carefully in this slick, half-frozen mud, but she was desperately hungry. If it weren't for the oldest mare, Midnight, she knew they could have gone at least a little faster. Every step down the mountainside brought them closer to new grass on the plains.

But Midnight was too old and too weak to go any

faster. They were all thin from the hard winter, but Midnight was the thinnest of all. Her bones were shoving against her skin.

Esperanza looked down the slope to the river. Its banks were still frozen. The sun wouldn't reach the canyon bottom until midday. It would be a while before spring truly arrived.

Esperanza shivered the skin on her flanks to scare off the mosquitoes. There weren't too many yet. They would get worse as the weather warmed—much worse.

Esperanza felt uneasy all the time now. Without the protection of a stallion and the guidance of a lead mare, this year's journey had been very different from their usual trek down the mountain.

Most of the herd was still miserable and hungry in their wintering valley. But six other horses had set out with Esperanza and her mother. The first night they had all sheltered together in a creek bottom. Esperanza had slept beside her best friend, Alicia.

The next morning, Esperanza's mother decided to

move on. The tall gray mare leading Alicia and her mother decided to stay and eat the willow growing beside the creek.

Esperanza knew this kind of scattering was usual for herds that had lost their stallions, but that didn't mean she liked it. She had followed her mother, of course, helpless to do more than answer Alicia's whinnies as the distance between them widened.

It had been six days since Esperanza had seen Alicia. She knew it was unlikely that she would ever see her again. The older mares stayed with groups of their own good friends. Their daughters were not quite old enough to make their own decisions.

Esperanza's mother's little band had three other mares in it . . . all of them much older than Esperanza. Gentle Midnight was so old, she had gray in the velvet fuzz on her muzzle.

The other two mares were both dark bays. They looked much alike, except that Aspen had a leaf-shaped white marking on her forehead while Willow's blood bay color was unmarred.

Esperanza loved all these mares. But she missed Alicia terribly. She let out a long breath and stared at her mother, daydreaming as they plodded along.

Alma was an unlikely leader. She was small-boned, a delicate beauty. She had a lovely face and her eyes were a deep coppery color. Her buckskin coat was still rough and thick from winter. But once the weather warmed, Esperanza knew, the fine gold-brown color would shine in the sun.

Esperanza rippled her skin. Her own coat was getting itchy. It wouldn't be long before they all began to shed. She had inherited half her mother's color—the shining gold. But her mother's mane and tail were black; her own were snowy white.

Esperanza pulled in a deep breath of the sweet, thin air. She would be so glad to be down out of the mountains this year. The herd always wintered in the mountains—the high valleys gave them shelter from the killing winds of the grassless winter plains. But this winter had been too long and too cold.

Esperanza couldn't wait to be out on the plains

again, with the spring grass coming up all around them. The plains' wildflowers and soft summer breezes would dim their memories of the terrible winter.

Esperanza's mother stopped abruptly on the narrow path, and Esperanza bumped into her. She tossed her head, startled out of her thoughts. Alma's tail twitched in irritation, but Esperanza knew her mother wasn't really angry. She was nervous.

Esperanza's mother had never in her life been the one likely to lead the herd. Every morning that they had been traveling, Alma had waited patiently for Aspen or Willow or Midnight to lead off. But they hadn't. None of them wanted the responsibility of deciding which way to go and where to stop. So Alma had done it. But Esperanza knew she was afraid—afraid of making a mistake.

It wouldn't take many days without food to kill Midnight. Wolves would notice her weakness now if Alma wasn't careful and clever at avoiding them. And the rest of them weren't much better off—they were not strong and any predator would be able to see that.

Esperanza watched her mother lift her head high, then thrust her muzzle into the air to try to scent danger. There was no real breeze, but the sun-warmed air was flowing gently uphill.

Esperanza waited, dreaming of deep grass and wide plains. Behind her, she heard Midnight tap the ground impatiently with one back hoof. Esperanza realized that unless her mother turned, she might not be able to tell who had done it.

Letting out a long, slow breath, Esperanza lowered her head—a relaxed gesture, touching her mother's hind leg lightly, just above the hock.

Alma twitched her ears, so Esperanza knew she had noticed the touch. But if Alma was worried about who was impatient with her stopping so often, she didn't show it. Her ears went straight back to their upright position.

Esperanza stood still, listening. There were no sounds except the usual ones, and the air was empty of dangerous scents. Still, her mother did not move.

Midnight ticked a hoof on the ground again. This time Aspen echoed the sound, the mud squelching as she shifted her weight.

Esperanza heard her mother let out a breath and knew that this time she *had* heard the sounds of impatience. But she still didn't move.

There *was* a reason, Esperanza realized abruptly, pulling in a long breath. Mountain lion. The wind carried news of lion. But the scent was pale and weak. The big cat was a long way off in distance and time. The scent was *old.*

Midnight gently nudged Esperanza from behind. Esperanza did not move. She couldn't—not until her mother decided it was safe.

When Alma finally started forward, Midnight blew out a long breath of relief. She had not meant to be rude, Esperanza knew. They were all hungry. Esperanza's stomach never stopped grinding. And they were all sick of eating bitter willow shoots. But Midnight's near-starvation over the winter was dangerously apparent. Her ribs were uneven ridges beneath her skin.

The next morning, Esperanza grazed beside a stand of cedar trees, pawing at the patches of dried grass the melting snow had revealed. It was filling but tasteless, and she struck at the ground with one forehoof. Her anger rose and she struck it a second time and a third.

Her mother looked up sharply, then stared at her for a moment. Esperanza knew why. Her furious pawing at the dead grass had made them all look up, wondering what was wrong.

It was rude to make the others think something was wrong when the only thing amiss was a hard winter and a late spring. Their own desperate grazing had been interrupted for nothing.

Esperanza dropped her head to apologize, tilting her ears backward just a little to show it wasn't all her fault. She was just hungry, and she wanted more than dried, thin grass. But they all did, she knew. She was sorry she had startled the other mares.

Once her mother had gone back to picking at the winter-browned grass, Esperanza shook herself. As much as she loved her mother and her mother's friends, she wished there was another horse her own age.

She missed Alicia terribly. Alicia would be as impatient as she was, she was sure. They could have stood together, apart from the others, restless and grumpy—and understanding each other. She loved Aspen, Willow, and especially Midnight. But they were her mother's friends. It was hard not to have a friend of her own.

Esperanza shook her mane, hard, then forced herself to concentrate on nibbling patiently at the tasteless brown grass.

Chapter Two

We traveled slowly, steadily, downhill. We never saw any mountain lions, though their scent was strong for a time. As we got lower and the sun warmed, we began finding new green grass. Midnight grazed constantly. Her jutting ribs began to disappear as she put on weight. We all listened constantly for danger. With so few of us—and without a stallion—we knew it was only a matter of time before we ran into something we couldn't handle.

One evening, Esperanza noticed her mother standing very close to Aspen. Midnight stood on Aspen's other side. Both the older mares were on watch, as always, their heads high, their ears moving. Aspen stood relaxed between them.

Esperanza realized something. The other mares were protective of Aspen because she was in foal. She would have a baby this year.

Esperanza looked at the mares and felt sad. Alicia would have stood watch for her like that someday. She would have done the same for Alicia.

The next morning, when the sky was just lightening to gray, Esperanza carefully eased herself away from the mares. She found a patch of bare earth and rolled on her back to loosen her brittle winter coat, then stood and shook, hard. She started off again, meaning to walk just a little ways, then come back.

Where the path led off to the east, she went straight, pushing her way through a budding plum thicket.

A sudden explosion of twigs and flying dirt caught Esperanza off guard. She leaped backward, then stood, stiff-legged, her heart thudding, her hooves dancing with nerves, ready to kick and strike.

But it was only a young doe. She stood very still, staring at Esperanza with wide brown eyes.

Esperanza lowered her head a little. The deer blinked. Then it sprang to one side, leaning low before it leaped in the opposite direction.

The invitation was unmistakable.

Esperanza ducked her head, then tossed her mane. It slapped against her neck and she shook it again, enjoying the sting against her skin.

She jumped to her side, her forelegs stiff and angled in front of her, letting the young doe know she had understood.

Moving together, they began to play.

Esperanza dodged as the doe sprang at her, rushing past. Then they both whirled in a tight circle and squared off again. They lowered their heads just enough to let each other know that there was no danger. This was just a game.

Esperanza leaped forward first this time. The doe jumped nearly straight up to avoid her, her cloven hooves flashing as she stuck out at the air. Esperanza spun around and pawed the ground.

The doe rushed at her, swerving to one side to leap past, then running in a tight, light-hoofed circle to come back.

Esperanza stood her ground. The doe plunged to a stop. They were both still for a moment, then the doe took off, fleet and fast.

Esperanza chased her, pounding along behind, circling the thickest brush. The doe soared over the same clumps, leaping gracefully.

Esperanza could not keep up, but the doe slowed just a little, pretending that she could not get away. Esperanza jumped a fallen tree, sailing over it just behind the doe.

The air was cool and crisp and the first sunlight of the day coated the mountainside with gold and rose light as they played.

It was Alma's frantic whinny that finally brought Esperanza up short. She dropped to a canter, then a trot, then she stopped and turned to look back uphill.

Not only was her own mother standing there, her ears flat in irritation, there was also an older doe a little ways behind her.

Breathing hard, Esperanza glanced at the young doe. Both their mothers had come to call them home.

The young doe's sides were heaving, too. But all the playfulness had left her posture. She stood steadily, flicking her long, deep, curved ears this way and that, her nose lifted to the wind.

Esperanza scented the rushing air.

Oh. Now she understood. She shook her mane and felt like a foolish foal. There was a vague scent of coyotes. They were not usually dangerous to a grown horse, but they were not to be ignored. It would scare Midnight to know they were this close when she was still so weak.

The young doe started uphill first, glancing back every few strides. Esperanza followed, wishing they had been able to play just a little longer.

As the days passed, the little band of mares kept traveling. The sunrises were nearly always painted with pink clouds and expanses of blue sky now. The flat gray skies of winter had gone.

The older mares all woke long after Esperanza did and it was hard to stand still every chilly morning, resisting the urge to move around, to stretch. She wanted to gallop, warming herself with every stride. But she didn't.

She knew the sudden sound of galloping hooves would startle the others awake and scare them. Then they would be angry with her—especially her mother. They were all uneasy enough without Esperanza making trouble.

So Esperanza stood still every morning, waiting for her mother and the others to awaken. It was so quiet just before dawn. In the grayish early light, the birds were not yet singing, and all the sounds of the night—even the rustling of mice—had stopped.

Everything was perfectly, strangely silent. It made Esperanza uneasy to feel so alone in the quiet world. She was always glad when the mares began to stir.

Every day brought them farther out of the cedar and pine forests and closer to the plains. Finally, one morning, when they set off, the ground was nearly level. It felt strange, after all of the time they had spent following a downhill slant.

By noon that day, they were no longer walking single file. There were so many paths through the brush that they often fanned out, walking almost abreast. Esperanza was glad. She was tired of feeling caught between her mother and Midnight on the narrow mountain trails.

None of the new trails seemed familiar. Esperanza realized that her mother had not taken their usual path downward. This was not the summer range the previous lead mare had always brought them to. Knowing that made Esperanza worry. Would they find enough grass and water here?

The sky overhead was a deep blue. As she had done the year before, Esperanza felt giddy beneath the prairie sky at first. It was so wide open. The sandy soil beneath her hooves was firm—perfect for a race. Esperanza longed for Alicia and her other friends to gallop with.

They came upon a wide canyon. For days they grazed along its rim. Then, one evening, they walked single file down a steep path to sleep in the leeward shelter of a red-rock cliff.

There was a shallow creek running along the bottom of the canyon. Along it grew cottonwood trees. They were just starting to leaf out, their buds yellow green and swollen.

Alma kept her little band close and led them cautiously. The first time they waded into the creek to drink, she stopped and listened, making them all wait for a long time before she led them forward into the soft muddy ground. If danger came while they floundered in the deep mud along the banks, they'd be helpless.

Holding them back, Alma stood watch almost like a stallion would, her head up, her ears swiveling back and forth, her nostrils flared wide to catch every scent.

When Alma finally went forward, Aspen followed at a trot. Her belly was bulging with her baby. She was always hungry and always thirsty.

Esperanza waded into the cool water. It wasn't very deep, not even rising to her knees, and even though the banks were muddy, the creek bottom was graveled, firm. The others waded in.

Midnight took a long draft of the cool water, then lifted her dripping muzzle and shook herself.

Esperanza saw the older mare glance up at the canyon's rim. For an instant her ears jerked forward, and Esperanza followed her gaze.

Suddenly there was a quick flash of movement and Esperanza stared, waiting for whatever had caught her eye to reappear. It didn't. But as they topped the canyon rim that morning and filed out onto the plains, Esperanza caught a faint scent. Horses. They were not alone.

Chapter Three

I know that Aspen was delighted about meeting the big herd. It was led by a strong stallion, and she felt safer than she had felt in a long time. My mother was glad, too, for her own reasons—she could turn over her unwanted responsibility to their lead mare. But we had been alone for such a long time, just the five of us, that I could only stare at the other horses, both excited and scared. By the time Strider came to meet me, I felt as awkward as a skinny-legged foal.

One morning Esperanza spotted horses on the horizon. They were grazing, moving slowly, fanned out over the plains.

Over the course of the day, they came closer, without hurrying. Esperanza watched them, lifting her head from the green grass so often that her mother finally came close and nudged her shoulder, then began to graze herself—as though teaching a foal how to eat.

Uneasy, knowing it was rude to stare at the others, Esperanza tried to graze, but it was hard. It was a *big* herd. The closer they came, the more she was aware that she had never been around this many horses—she had never *seen* this many horses in one place before.

There were so many yearlings that they stood off to one side, playing and grazing, barely interested in the new mares. The mares with foals formed their own group, too.

The stallion pranced around his herd, stopping to graze off and on, but always moving, his head up, alert and protective. There was no wind. He lifted his head, trying to scent them, but then he shook his mane in irritation. It was impossible because the air was too still. He would have to come closer.

Esperanza watched him. He was a tall, handsome grulla, that odd cedar-bark color between brown and gray. When they finally got close enough to scent each other, Esperanza saw him gather himself, his muscles tense as he arched his neck. He pawed at the ground, squealing a high-pitched call that echoed against the distant hills. When there was no answer, he turned, all his posturing relaxed as he watched them, his head high.

Esperanza understood. He was finally sure that there was no stallion with them, that he would not have to fight. He approached them cautiously, walking respectfully toward Alma first, sensing correctly that she was the lead mare of this group.

Esperanza stood still, keeping her head respectfully low. Aspen and the others were being just as polite.

The mares and young stallions were all looking at them now, watching and waiting to see what

Alma would do. Even the yearlings had looked up.

The stallion reached out, allowing Alma to scent his breath and skin. Esperanza could smell a sharp familiar scent from where she stood, a little way off from her mother. Not only was the stallion the color of cedar bark, but the scent of cedar clung to his coat as well. Had this herd just come down from the mountains?

Cedar walked around Alma. She stood tall, but Esperanza knew her mother was probably trembling. She was shy. Still, she held her ground, and when Cedar reached out again, she extended her muzzle toward his.

At that moment a mare came forward from the herd, a half-grown stallion following her. The mare was shining, jet black and so was her son. He had a bold, striding gait.

The young stallion had no white markings at all. Even his mane and tail were as dark as a night sky. He followed his mother partway, then stopped when she made her way straight toward Alma.

Esperanza watched as the black mare walked past

Cedar without so much as pausing. It was obvious that she was not afraid of him; she did not ask his permission.

Esperanza watched her. Alma lowered her own head, to show respect. The black mare came close.

Esperanza held her breath. This mare's decision to accept them all without resistance would make all the difference in the world. Without it, they would have to hang along the edges of the herd for weeks or months, waiting to feel welcomed. Or maybe they would simply have to move on alone.

Esperanza felt her heart sink at the idea of having to leave them. A big herd with a strong stallion would mean safety, an end to worrying and standing lookout with her mother. It would mean *friends*.

Esperanza watched as the black mare and her own mother exchanged breath, touching muzzles lightly. All the others were watching, even Cedar. He stood off a little ways, his ears up, glancing toward each horizon every few seconds.

There wasn't going to be any trouble, Esperanza was sure. Her mother was shy and polite. She

wouldn't try to remain in the role of lead mare—
she didn't like it. And it looked like the lead mare
was calm and at ease—almost friendly.

Esperanza allowed herself to look at the herd,
paying more attention now that she was a little less
nervous about being driven off.

There were a lot of mares her age, and a number of young stallions, too. The foals all looked
strong and healthy, their long legs skinny and awkward as they hid behind their mothers.

The lead mare's son came forward a few steps,
using the same long-striding pace, then stopping, his
head held high. Esperanza watched him. He moved
as though the world were his. Strider. She hoped
they could be friends.

Esperanza glanced at Aspen. She was looking on
eagerly, her ears forward. Esperanza realized that
she had been lonely, too, in her own way. There
were a number of mares in the herd who looked as
close to foaling as she did.

Abruptly Esperanza noticed that the young black
stallion was looking directly at her. She lowered her

head to be polite. This herd had not accepted her yet, after all. And Strider's mother was the lead mare. Being respectful was important.

Esperanza wondered later if she had been staring rudely at Strider. Probably. She had been fascinated by his gait, his posture.

Strider's mother finally turned her attention to Midnight, then Aspen, then to Willow. Then she sniffed at Esperanza, her manner calm and friendly. Once she had greeted each of them, she turned and took her place with the big herd again.

Then, without further ceremony, she began to walk. As she moved on, the others followed, ranging widely behind her. Esperanza tossed her head. Had it really been that easy to be accepted?

Esperanza let her breath out. They had found a home! After she had wanted one for so long, it had all seemed too easy. She stood still out of habit, waiting for her mother to lead off. When she finally did, Esperanza fell in behind her.

Strider was moving forward at about the same pace as she was, Esperanza noticed. She stopped to graze for a moment, tearing lightly at the fresh new grass. She chewed as she walked, then stopped again.

Glancing sideways, Esperanza saw that Strider had stopped, too. He grazed easily, seeming to be completely relaxed, even though he lifted his head high every few moments to look around.

Esperanza kept watching him from the corner of her eye. His black coat shone nearly blue in the sun. He was strong and handsome, but that wasn't why Esperanza could not look away.

He really did walk like his mother did, as though the earth and sky belonged to him—as though there were nothing he needed to fear.

Esperanza moved forward a few steps, then stopped to graze again. Strider stopped, too. He angled his direction and grazed along, coming closer to her.

Suddenly shy, Esperanza veered off, walking at an angle. She kept her ears pitched backward to hear if Strider was following her. He was.

Feeling silly about trying to get away from him,

Esperanza waded into a thicket of buck brush without thinking, then was too embarrassed to stop in the center of it when she realized what she was doing. She just kept walking. She could hear Strider as he stopped at the edge of the thicket.

Just then, from right beneath her hooves, a frantic rustling rose from the leaves. An instant later, something shot out, bumping against her right foreleg.

Startled, Esperanza leaped backward and slammed into Strider's side. He braced himself in time and held them both up.

Esperanza saw the jackrabbit she had startled, its black tail bobbing as it tore off, heading toward someplace safe, someplace where horses knew enough to look where they were walking.

Esperanza felt a warm touch on her shoulder.

She turned to see Strider looking at her steadily. He didn't seem to think she was foolish for being startled. He was just trying to let her know everything was all right.

Esperanza shook her mane and reached out to let

him take her breath as she inhaled his. After what seemed like a long time, he went back to grazing, staying close beside Esperanza, as though they had been friends all their lives.

Chapter Four

*S*trider *was so calm and confident. It was simply the way he was. He had spent his whole life following his mother as she decided where the herd should stop, where they would be safe for the night. He was used to being alert for danger all the time. He kept watch like a grown stallion already.*

Esperanza realized something on the fourth day they traveled with Cedar's herd. These horses had a big homeland—and they needed it. There were so many of them that they grazed the grass low very quickly. They had to keep moving almost constantly.

As they walked through the long spring days, Esperanza saw her mother grazing closer and closer to Strider's mother, until the two of them were walking nearly side by side most days.

Esperanza was glad her mother had made a new friend so quickly. Old Midnight often walked with them as well. Willow and Aspen had new companions too. The herd simply made room for all of them.

One morning, Aspen's foal was born, a lovely, light gray filly. By noon she was walking clumsily. Esperanza met her formally, trading breath, then moved aside so Alma and Willow and Midnight could take their turns.

The herd drifted slowly until evening. By the following morning, the newborn scrambled up with the rest of the horses at dawn, and except for a nap near noontime that slowed the herd's progress for a while, she kept up very well.

A few days later, another foal was born. Aspen and her baby began walking close to the new mother.

After a few days, the foals began playing together, running circles around their mothers.

During the cool morning hours, the herd usually traveled briskly. Then, by midmorning, Strider's mother usually slowed the pace so that they could graze more than they walked.

Esperanza saw her mother standing watch as she had done all winter long, watching the horizon as the others grazed. Strider's mother did the same thing. Cedar seemed to approve.

He often touched Alma with his muzzle as he passed. He greeted Aspen, Willow, and Midnight politely as well. He always acknowledged Esperanza as he passed her, even though she was so young.

Esperanza knew they were very lucky to have found a herd as big and as friendly as this one.

As the pleasant days passed, Esperanza saw her mother begin to put on weight. Alma was able to graze more now that she was not the only one standing watch.

One bright morning, Strider galloped around in a tight circle, bucking and kicking at the sky. Then he flattened out into a gallop, celebrating the morning. His hooves thudded against the ground as he swept past, and Esperanza leaped into a canter without thinking.

Galloping hard, Esperanza followed Strider as he veered outward, enlarging his circles for the sake of a chase. She could almost catch him, but not quite.

After a few minutes, several of the younger mares and stallions joined them and Esperanza pounded over the ground, her tail streaming behind her. She felt wonderful! The sage burst into pungent clouds of scent as she galloped through it.

The gallop went on and on. . . .

By the time Esperanza dropped back into a trot, she and Strider were the only two still running. Esperanza glanced sideward at Cedar, but he was preoccupied with grooming one of the pregnant mares. Her eyes were closed in appreciation as he chewed burs from her mane.

Strider's mother didn't seem to mind the playful galloping either. She whinnied gently as Strider passed. He dropped back to a walk and stopped to exchange a greeting with his mother. They both raised their heads, tilting them, nipping at each other like two colts playing.

Esperanza kicked up her heels and turned a tight circle, then galloped a wider arc before she plunged to a stop to watch Strider and his mother. When Strider's mother stepped away to lead the herd onward, Esperanza rejoined Strider.

Both of them were still breathing hard from the long gallop. Esperanza touched Strider's shoulder with her muzzle. He loved to gallop as much as she did! Esperanza let out a long breath. Maybe Alicia had found a new friend, too, wherever she had ended up. Esperanza hoped she had.

Strider walked beside her all that day, and the next. The weather was warming up, and the wildflowers grew in clumps where there was enough water to sustain them. The snow was long gone, and the sandy soil did not hold moisture long. If the summer rains came soon, the wildflowers would last a long time.

Esperanza grazed beside Strider, more content

with every day that passed. Cedar kept a peaceful herd. Strider's mother managed things so well that there was little reason for any of the horses *not* to get along.

Cedar stood apart, usually on higher ground than the herd, if he could. Esperanza glanced up at him a dozen times a day. He was always alert, always facing into the wind to learn what he could from the scents it carried.

The wind often came up in the afternoons. One day it swelled into a stiff breeze. Esperanza loved it, loved the smell of the sage and the wildflowers it carried. As she walked, she heard her mother nicker and turned to look at her.

Alma was standing not too far from Strider's mother, but she was facing the opposite direction. Her ears were pricked forward stiffly, and Esperanza knew she was listening.

Out of long habit, Esperanza turned in the same direction and tried to hear danger, if there was any. The buffeting of the breeze made it impossible.

After a few minutes, Alma fell back to grazing

and Esperanza relaxed. There was no danger. Her mother had just taken longer to decide they were safe because the wind drowned out any distant sounds.

Strider walked beside Esperanza as they moved forward. Rounding the base of a bluff, they picked their way through thick sagebrush.

The horses on all sides of Esperanza were slowing, making their way through the brittle, silvery stalks. The rising wind whistled through the stiff leaves.

Esperanza glanced sideways. Aspen's little gray filly was struggling hard to keep her head above the brush. She was lifting her tiny hooves high, almost rearing as she pushed through the sage. Aspen kept looking back, but she couldn't really help.

Suddenly the filly jerked to a stop, her head high, her ears pinned flat against her head.

Esperanza hesitated midstep, and she saw Strider glance her way. She turned slightly, watching the gray filly.

Abruptly, Aspen whirled, whinnying, her eyes wide and rimmed in white. She backed up, her head low. Then, without warning, she flinched backward.

Strider lunged forward, plunging through the sagebrush toward the frightened foal. Once he was close, he reared, driving both forehooves straight downward, his full weight behind the strike.

Esperanza came closer, and the sharp, ugly scent of a rattlesnake came to her on the swift wind. She skidded to a stop as Strider rose a second time.

Esperanza saw the fear—and the courage—in his eyes as he came down again, his hooves thudding on the creature's coiled body. At that instant, Cedar's angry call pierced the wind.

Esperanza turned toward the sound of Cedar's furious squeal. The stallion swept past her in a blur, his head thrust forward and his teeth bared. Aspen leaped aside, too, and led her filly out of the way.

Esperanza caught her breath. Cedar charged straight at Strider, reaching out to bite at his flank when he whirled to get away. For a long moment, Cedar chased him, slashing the air with his teeth, then he slid to a stop and spun back to Aspen and her foal.

As Strider galloped toward Esperanza, she looked past him to see Cedar rearing high, making a show of trampling the already dead snake. Aspen had taken her foal back into the herd. Alma stood close, comforting her.

Cedar trotted back toward the mares, his neck arched proudly. Aspen lowered her head, thanking him for making sure her foal was safe. Some of the mares moved closer, forming a loose circle around Cedar.

Esperanza touched Strider's muzzle with her own as he stopped before her. He had only wanted to help Aspen's foal. But that was Cedar's role, not his. Cedar would never stand for any of the younger stallions taking over his responsibilities—not without a fight.

Esperanza knew that once Cedar was old, one of the young stallions would fight him and win. But not yet. Not for a long time. Cedar was young still, and he was very strong.

Esperanza shook her mane and stood close to Strider. He was still breathing hard, trembling with fear at the snake—and from Cedar's fury.

Cedar's reaction seemed unfair, yet Esperanza had known that this was coming. Older stallions never tolerated younger ones once they began to grow up and want a herd of their own. Cedar would not forget. Esperanza knew it would not be long before the older stallion drove Strider out of the herd. The thought made her heart ache.

Chapter Five

*W*e moved across rough country for a long time. The soil was rocky and the land was broken with bands of reddish stone. Midnight grew sleek and healthy and Aspen's foal grew graceful and strong. After our terrible winter, all was well. All the horses in Cedar's big herd seemed content. Except for Strider. And because he wasn't, I could not be.

Just before dawn, it sprinkled a little. Not enough to really wet the soil, but it settled the dust. Esperanza shivered, enjoying it. Strider shook his mane and stamped a forehoof. Esperanza knew what he was thinking. It would be a wonderful morning to gallop when the sun came up.

She hesitated.

Strider nudged her gently and stamped playfully again.

Esperanza lowered her head, then tossed her mane. Maybe, if they walked away from the others—just a little ways—their galloping wouldn't bother Cedar. The stallion had been keeping an eye on Strider ever since he had shown such courage trying to protect Aspen's foal.

Esperanza led off cautiously and Strider followed. There was a little rise to the east. The sky above it was lightening, a gray blue just barely lighter than the rest of the sky.

Two eagles drifted in circles in the growing light. Esperanza could hear their high wind-torn whistles as they called to each other.

It was going to be a glorious morning. The rain-softened air was delicious, and Esperanza pulled in a deep breath as they started up the slope.

As always, she tasted the air, searching it for signs of danger. She stared into the dawn-dusk as well, wary for any signs of movement, any flashes of motion that might mean danger was near. Esperanza knew without looking that Strider was doing the same thing.

Behind them she heard one of the mares nicker sleepily to her colt, soothing it.

Esperanza put her ears back to listen. There was no further sound. If any of the horses had noticed them leaving, they didn't care.

Strider glanced at her. Esperanza brought her ears forward and walked a little faster. After a time, she lifted herself into a trot. They were far enough away now. Their hoofbeats were muffled by the summer dust.

As they topped the rise, the clouds along the eastern horizon were flushing into gray and rose. A gentle breeze had kicked up, bringing a bouquet of rain scents along with it. In the sagebrush below the two of them, the rustling of mice and quail was beginning. The creatures of the land were waking up. Esperanza stood close to Strider, waiting.

The sky flared from rose into orange and pink; the gold shot through the edges of the clouds. And at that instant Strider reared, scraping at the sky with his forehooves. Then he dropped down to lunge into a gallop. Esperanza was right behind him.

They thundered out onto the prairie, carving a long, curving path through the sage, racing each other as the sun's first rays flashed over the land, a fan of amber light that made everything seem bright and new.

As they came down a slope and headed for a creek that curved along a bluff, Esperanza saw something big moving in the half-light. It was unusual for a bear to be this far out on the plains, and it took her a moment to realize that was what she was seeing.

Astonished, she slid to a halt. Already in the lead, Strider swept onward, deafened by the sound of his own hooves, the sunrise celebration pounding in his veins. Esperanza whinnied, frantic. There had been no scent, no trace of bear on the wind.

She whinnied again, throwing her head high to make the warning carry. This time Strider heard her. He glanced back, swiveling his ears to hear her better, and he slowed.

Esperanza whinnied once more, realizing why they had not smelled the bear, even though it was upwind. The wet earth and sage had masked all but the faintest trace.

She could smell the musky bear-scent now—now that it did them no good at all. She stared at the bear rising onto its hind legs. It was then that she saw the smaller shapes. She caught her breath. Strider had accidentally gotten between the bear and her cubs!

Strider plunged to a stop, his ears pinned back tightly, his teeth bared as the bear started toward him. The early sunlight cast long, angular shadows that striped the ground with dark shapes. Esperanza was sure he hadn't noticed the cubs behind him.

The bear charged at Strider, swiping at the air with its massive paws. Strider retreated, his hooves clattering—but in the wrong direction. He very near-ly stumbled over the cubs.

The bear roared her rage, lunging at him as he leaped away from the baby bears.

Terrified for Strider, Esperanza burst into a gal-lop. Acting against every instinct, she headed straight toward the mother bear.

Strider was wheeling around. The cubs were try-ing to get to their mother just as he was fighting to get *away* from her. But Esperanza knew that he couldn't outrun her over a short distance—not in the open like this.

Esperanza squealed a warning as she got close, and the charging bear glanced her way. Its eyes widened. It had not expected her to interfere, she was sure. A mare would protect her foal. A stallion would protect his herd. But few mares would come to the rescue of a friend.

And maybe, Esperanza realized as she veered close to the bear to distract it, it was the most fool-ish thing she could have done. Maybe she and Strider would both die now. Bears rarely attacked horses, but any mother would protect her young—and any bear this big could kill a horse in a single blow.

Esperanza kicked her heels close to the bear, then threw herself to the side to stay clear of her raking claws. One swipe could cripple her forever, Esperanza knew. She veered away, then wheeled back, galloping close again.

Angered, the bear turned its full attention to Esperanza.

Strider took advantage of the momentary distraction to wrench himself around. He squealed, heading back toward the cubs.

The mother bear saw what he was doing and turned toward him again, ignoring Esperanza's whinnies. Esperanza tore at the earth, digging in with her hooves in as she hurled herself forward.

Again, a second before the bear caught up with Strider, she swung close and made it swerve to lash out at her.

Strider arced away from the cubs and Esperanza followed him. The bear, facing her cubs now, saw that they were safe. She roared at the intruders, then slowed to an amble.

Esperanza and Strider raced back over the sagebrush and rain-beaded grass.

Strider led the way in a long arc back to the herd, making sure the bear would not follow—even at a distance—before he dropped back to a trot.

Esperanza slowed with him, her breath coming in short gasps.

A sudden whinny startled her. Cedar was prancing toward them, his neck arched, his eyes fierce. They slowed again, then stopped as Cedar came closer.

Strider lowered his head, keeping his eyes down, too. Esperanza hoped that Cedar could see the respect and courtesy Strider was giving him.

The grulla stallion plunged to a stop before them. He reared, striking at the air, then pivoted and kicked, missing Strider's face by the length of a sage blossom.

Esperanza held very still, her legs trembling from the flight, the fear ... and now this.

The whole herd was looking at them, watching as Cedar pranced and postured, acting the way he would if Strider were some strange stallion approaching his herd. Maybe he thought Strider had meant to run away, taking her with him. Whatever he thought, what he wanted now was a fight. He would defeat Strider and drive him out if he could.

Esperanza could see her mother, and Strider's, standing with the others. Alma could not help with this, Esperanza knew. Nor could Strider's mother. Stallions had always fought. It was their way.

Without warning, Cedar reared again, then pivoted to kick his heels once more, coming so close to Strider's face that Strider flinched backward. Strider did not run, but he didn't accept the challenge, either. He stood still, forcing Cedar to decide whether to fight or back down.

As suddenly as he had attacked, Cedar stopped. He turned his back on Strider and trotted back to the herd, his neck arched, his hooves flashing.

At that instant, Strider's mother neighed urgently and led off. The tension in the air dissolved as the herd stretched out over the prairie. Esperanza watched them following Strider's mother—and her own—toward the day's grazing. She and Strider fell into line near the middle of the herd, keeping to the edge.

Chapter Six

I smelled wolves one morning, but it was faint. Unless one of the foals strayed from the herd—or a lone mare was caught in the open, they would probably chase mice and rabbits as they usually did in the summer. Still, the memories of our terrible winter made me grateful to be part of such a big, strong herd. I knew I would like it much less if Cedar drove Strider away. I also knew that was certain to happen sooner or later. I feared it would not be long.

The early summer rains finally began. Nearly every afternoon, clouds boiled up in the west and sailed across the sky. The rain didn't always fall, but the horses could smell it in the air. When it did, the break in the dry heat was exciting. The younger horses bucked and galloped in circles around the herd, enjoying the sudden coolness.

Thunder and dry-strike lightning sometimes drove the whole herd into a mad, fearful gallop. Whenever that happened, Cedar was frantic, trying to keep them all together.

Strider and Esperanza began traveling a little way off to one side of the herd. They were never too far from the mares as they fanned out to graze, but they were out of Cedar's way when the storms rolled through and the mares began to gallop in circles.

Late one afternoon Esperanza smelled another storm coming. The scent of rain-bruised sage was unmistakable, but it carried another, unfamiliar scent with it as well.

Esperanza did not recognize the scent—it was like nothing she had ever smelled before. She watched her mother as the storm appeared on the horizon. Alma seemed uneasy. The whole herd did.

Afternoon passed into evening as Esperanza watched the storm rage its way across the prairie toward them. The leading edge of the clouds was dark, almost black. The column of rain that spilled out of them was a gray curtain across the land. This was no ordinary summer rain.

With the storm coming closer every second, the horses cantered and bucked. Cedar ran a circular course around them all, driving any stragglers back into the herd. Esperanza and Strider moved closer on their own, before Cedar had to force them.

The wind rose sharply. The mares gathered themselves into a tight knot, their eyes glittering fearfully in the flickering, blue white light of the electrical storm.

Alma made her way through the milling mares to stand beside her daughter. Somehow, that scared Esperanza more than anything else. Her mother had not stood near to comfort her in a long time. It made her feel even more like a frightened foal. And still the wind rose.

The rain fell like no rain Esperanza had ever

known. It was driven sideways by the screaming winds, hitting the horses like pebbles, stinging their skin.

Strider stood on one side of Esperanza and her mother stood close on the other. Still, she was terrified. Strider's mother neighed reassuringly now and then, but her voice was scattered by the gale.

Esperanza dreaded the coming of night. The darker it got, the more terrifying the lightning became. Ragged silver veins of light laced the sky overhead, and everything below was lit an eerie blue white. Then darkness swallowed the world again and thunder shook the ground.

When the silver-blue light brightened again, Esperanza tried to spot Aspen and her foal. It was impossible. The horses were standing too close together, their heads too low. She caught one glimpse of Midnight when the gray-muzzled mare tossed her head, then the lightning winked out and thunder slammed at them from above.

The next flash of light brought a vision so strange, Esperanza was sure she would never understand it.

It terrified her. There was a dark column coming toward them, tall as a mountain, high enough to touch the belly of the clouds. It was as though a gigantic whirling tree had somehow risen from the earth. And it was howling, roaring, headed straight toward them.

Esperanza trembled and waited.

Even her mother was shaking in fear.

And still the wind rose.

The wind blew so hard that it seemed to Esperanza there was nothing in the world *but* wind. It had claws and teeth, and it tore at Esperanza's mane and tail. The lightning flashed red, and she realized her eyes were closed, shut against the stinging sand, the flying twigs and pebbles. Then, somehow, she was galloping away from it—or trying to.

The darkness rushed and moaned around her. Strider was by her side. They kept bumping into each other as they struggled to find a way out of the crushing roar of the wind.

It was terribly dangerous to gallop in the dark. But Esperanza galloped anyway. The wind shrieked like it would never stop, like the world would end in a screaming whirl of wind. Esperanza fled blindly, feeling the rise and fall of Strider's shoulder brushing against her own.

Time slid past them, as confused and violent as the wind. The night seemed endless. Twice they veered, changing direction when the spinning column of wind came at them again. Esperanza lost her footing on a slope and fell, rolling and sliding, then somehow scrambling her way upright to find Strider waiting for her.

They kept pounding along, straining to outrace the wind, until Esperanza's legs felt too heavy to lift. She finally slowed, not because she wanted to, but because she had to. As they dropped to a canter, then a trot, Strider labored onward beside her, his hooves churning, his sides heaving.

The wind had let up a little, Esperanza realized. It was still terrible, but its claws had been worn down, scraping at the earth. The sky was getting lighter, too, beginning to turn gray. The long night was coming to an end. Esperanza stared at the horizon, then at Strider.

Startled, she realized that he was standing still. They both were. When had they stopped? Esperanza shook her mane wearily and blinked. Strider had a long bloody scrape on one leg. What had done it? A rock? Her hooves? They had galloped so close together for so long. . . .

Esperanza was grateful neither of them was more hurt. She moved, swaying forward, then back. Her right foreleg was a little sore. She remembered falling and sliding downhill, and scrambling upright again. How far had they run? She stared at the brightening horizon. She was eager for morning. The whole terrifying night was blurred in her mind.

As the sun rose above the clouds, lighting the earth, Esperanza looked at the countryside around her.

The wind had knocked the sagebrush flat. It had torn cottonwood trees limb from limb, scattering their branches like weed straws. The very earth seemed changed, all the dust of summer scoured away.

Strider lowered his head to touch Esperanza gently. She sidled closer and realized her whole body was shaking. Strider took a single step and she nickered anxiously, afraid to have him move away from her.

Strider lifted his head, scenting the wind. Esperanza forced herself to do the same. The strange smell was gone. Had it been the storm itself? She only knew that if she ever smelled it again, she would start galloping instantly—she would outrun the strange, killing winds next time.

Strider took another step. Esperanza followed, her legs aching and weak. He led her slowly forward. She stumbled twice, barely able to walk. She wasn't hurt; it was as though the wind had blown away her courage, her *will*.

Soon Strider stopped. They were beside a creek. Esperanza lowered her head and drank the cool water. It was brownish. The wind had battered it, too, stirring up the mud.

As she lifted her head, she realized something. They were alone, completely. No other horses were anywhere near. She turned, looking, scenting the air. Hadn't any of the herd ended up fleeing in the same direction she and Strider had taken? Where was her mother?

Esperanza shook herself. The wind was still blowing, but it wasn't that strong anymore. They could travel. The herd couldn't be that far away. All they had to do was retrace their own path. She turned, facing away from the rising sun. She wanted to find her mother and Aspen and . . .

Strider lunged forward and stood before her, his head low.

Esperanza stopped, confused. She tried to start forward and he stopped her again. Because of the wind, because her legs and her lungs hurt, because she had galloped all night and was exhausted, it took her a long time to understand.

Even if they could find the herd, Strider didn't want to go back. He didn't want *her* to go back.

Esperanza tried twice more, but then she gave up. Strider was right. It was time. Cedar would soon have driven him out. And she would have wanted to leave with him. She would miss her mother, but Alma would understand.

Esperanza drew in a long breath. She and Strider needed to find their own homeland now.

Chapter Seven

I t was as though one life had ended and
another had begun. I was afraid at first. I
longed to head back to the herd. But I trusted
Strider. He kept watch while I slept, then I
would listen and watch while he dozed. I began
to feel better as the days passed. One morning
we galloped together through a cool dawn mist.

Esperanza thought finding their own homeland
would be easy. After all, she had always lived in
places where lead mares found water holes and
grass. She had always known where to find fine

sand to roll in during the summer and stands of willow in the winter—and every other thing a horse could need.

But as they traveled, she learned something. Not all land held these things.

The first few days, they found grass, but no water. Then they followed a clear, deep creek for days, but there was so little grass growing next to it that Esperanza began to feel almost sick with hunger.

One morning, when Strider started off, Esperanza stood still, lifting her head to scent the dawn breeze. Strider stopped and looked back at her. She lifted her head a little higher, ignoring his impatient nickering. She had caught a faint scent that she wanted to find again.

Strider nickered a second time. Esperanza usually let him lead the way, and she could tell that he was both puzzled and irritated. Still she did not move. This was important. She waited for the tiniest of breezes to stir the air.

There.

It was as faint as a moon shadow, but she was certain. She could smell green grass. She whinnied at Strider.

He shook his mane and started to turn around to lead off again, but Esperanza whinnied once more. Then she set off in her own direction, following the wind scent.

Strider stood still for a long moment. Esperanza glanced back at him. He was a good leader and she trusted him. But she could smell grass, and grass was what they needed so desperately. It was time for him to trust her. Strider shook his head once more, then trotted to catch up.

The country turned browner as they went, but the whisper scent of green grass was still in the wind. So Esperanza kept moving, following it. Strider stayed by her side.

The next watering place they came to had a strong, terrible odor, and Esperanza barely wet her muzzle before she lifted her head and shook it to rid herself of the sour taste.

They went on. They looked for good water all

that day, but couldn't find any. That night they slept beneath the stars, without even a cottonwood to shelter them. It felt dangerous, and Esperanza barely dozed. She stared into the darkness, listening, all night.

When the sun came up again, the land looked even bleaker than it had the evening before.

Esperanza raised her head. The faint smell of green grass was still in the breeze, nearly hidden by the smells of dust and heat. She followed it, hope rising in her heart. Strider followed without hesitation this time.

Esperanza traveled as fast as she could, but her empty belly made it difficult. Midday, with the summer sun glaring off the earth, Esperanza knew they had to find shelter from the heat. But there was no shelter.

In the afternoon, crossing the endless brown country, Esperanza almost lost her courage. What if she had made a mistake about the grass scent? Maybe she was leading them into more dry country.

Esperanza ticked a front hoof against a rock and

nearly stumbled. Maybe they had been foolish not to go back to the herd. She shook her mane. She knew she was just scared. She wasn't sorry she had followed Strider. But they had to find water and food soon.

Esperanza knew that horses sometimes died on sun-burned prairies. Strider moved up to walk beside her. He never faltered. His courage lifted Esperanza's heart, and she kept going.

A spattering rain that evening washed away the strong dusty scent that had filled the wind. By the next morning, the smell of green grass was stronger, easier to follow. Esperanza felt her spirits lifting, and she tried to travel a little faster. Strider matched her pace and walked close to her. Then, midday, the wind shifted and the scent disappeared.

Esperanza knew they had come too far to turn back. They would never live through another crossing of the dry plain. She had no choice, so she kept going in the same direction. There was no scent to guide her now, so she kept them on course by the sight of the distant blue mountains. One snowy peak marked the right direction.

Strider stayed close beside her all day. His head was up, alert for enemies, for danger of any kind. Esperanza glanced at him often, grateful to have such a brave stallion beside her. He was too weak to fight, but he would still try to protect her, she was sure.

Finally, as evening drew close, they came upon some hills, and Esperanza saw the sloping entrance to a little valley. It was shallow and long, flanked by a gradual ridge on one side and a steep clay bluff on the other.

Esperanza couldn't scent the grass; the wind was blowing the wrong way. But this close, she could see it. Tired, weak from days of hunger, she broke into a shuffling trot.

Strider followed, then came up beside her as they waded into the grass. He touched her neck with his muzzle, thanking her for bringing them though the dry land. Then he dropped his head to graze. Esperanza joined him, nearly dizzy with relief and the smells of damp earth and lush grass.

The ground beneath their hooves gave with their weight, and Esperanza knew that this place was probably flooded in early spring. But now it was just damp enough to grow grass under the hot summer sun.

Staying close together, they ate fast, snatching up huge mouthfuls, their jaws grinding constantly. The grass was so lush that it quenched the worst of Esperanza's thirst as it filled her belly. When she had finally quieted her hunger, she lifted her head, still chewing, and looked around for the first time.

It was a little cooler in the valley, and there were spreading cottonwoods and sumac at the far end. She lowered her head to the soil and breathed in slowly. It smelled sweet.

The wind was still blowing from behind them, and Esperanza studied the cottonwoods for a long time before she started toward them.

She knew that a valley this nice likely had some animals living in it already. The wind was blowing the wrong way to tell her if anything dangerous was back in the trees. But they would have to find out before they decided to sleep here. Strider hesitated, then caught up and walked a little ahead of her, his head up and his ears forward.

Esperanza slowed, then stopped as they neared the trees. She could not hear or see anything, but the shade was deep—the shadows could be hiding anything. The sun was lowering in the sky and the shadows would only get deeper.

The trees would be the safest place to sleep—if no predator was sheltering there. Esperanza would be unwilling to pass beneath the low branches once it was dark. Maybe they should just sleep in the open and wait until full sunlight to explore the trees.

Then she heard a muted sound. Water. There was a creek running behind the stand of trees. The grass had eased her thirst, but she still wanted water. She glanced at Strider.

He arched his neck and took a step forward, clearly willing to risk danger for a drink of water. Esperanza glanced around, still feeling cautious.

Strider seemed to read her thoughts. He led the way forward, but angled to the edge of the copse of trees, going around them rather than beneath them.

Esperanza followed.

As they made their way around the last of the spreading trees, she caught an even stronger scent of water. She could tell that Strider had smelled it, too, because he walked faster, his head high.

When she saw the sparkle of the little pond glinting through the grass, Esperanza let out a long breath. They could stay here awhile. They could rest and eat. And maybe this would be the right place. Perhaps this valley—if it was big enough— would make a good homeland.

At that instant, a thin thread of a completely unfamiliar scent came on the air. Esperanza nearly stumbled. It was entirely unknown to her. She had no idea if it meant danger or not.

Before she could react, the barely stirring air slid past her and the scent was gone. She looked at Strider. He had not scented anything, she was sure. He didn't slow his pace. Maybe she had been mistaken—maybe the odd scent had been a mixture of scents. It had come and gone so quickly that she wasn't really sure.

Esperanza hurried to catch up, following him to the edge of the pond. They lowered their muzzles into the sweet pond water and drank side by side.

Chapter Eight

*I*t was a beautiful valley. We slept down-wind of the trees that night in the tall grass beyond the pond. The morning was bright and perfect. I thought we had found our homeland. But we had not. I have never understood what we saw that day. I don't think I ever will.

The sunrise seemed late, coming over a high bluff to the east. But it was bright—not a single cloud in the sky. Esperanza woke slowly. She had been watchful for the first part of the night, but after enough hours of complete silence, and no repetition of the odd scent, she had fallen fast asleep.

Strider woke suddenly, pulling in a startled breath, and Esperanza knew he had slept deeply, too. It was unlike either of them to be so careless. They had been exhausted.

Esperanza felt her hunger rising the minute she was fully awake. It was as though the deep green grass were calling to her, like a friendly neigh on the morning air.

Strider did not object when she led the way to the edge of the pond and drank, then started back down the valley. By the time they reached the edge of the grass, he was beside her.

For a long time, Esperanza ate fast again. The grass was amazingly fresh for midsummer. It was still as juicy and sweet as first-spring grass.

Strider ate intently, too, and Esperanza was glad that he was in no hurry to explore the valley. Her hunger had taken days to become desperate, and she knew it would take some time to calm it entirely.

It was the high, trailing whistle of an eagle overhead that made them both look up and realize that the sun had climbed the sky. It was now nearly straight above them.

Esperanza shook her mane and sidled close to Strider. He leaned toward her, his breath sweet with the grass. They stood close for a few seconds, and Esperanza felt completely safe for the first time since the wind had torn them from the herd.

Esperanza shuddered at the memory of the sky-ripping wind. She pulled in a slow breath. The air was so completely still, so soft with moisture here, it was hard to imagine that any wind could ever have been that violent.

Side by side, they walked back up the long valley, heading for the shade of the cottonwoods. The spongy soil dried—and the grass thinned—as they went. Esperanza heard frogs croak sleepily in the pond beyond the trees as they got closer. She could hear small birds in the tree branches, too. These were good signs. When there was danger, the birds usually flew—or hid quietly.

The cottonwoods were still, their shiny leaves deep green. Strider stood, scenting the air, then walked forward slowly.

Esperanza followed him. Passing from sun to shade, she blinked as her eyes adjusted.

The earth beneath the trees was hard, as though hooved animals had come here often—even though she saw no hoofprints. Esperanza lifted her head, expecting to scent deer. Instead, the odd scent she had noticed the night before filled her nostrils. It was faint, but distinct. She stopped, her head up, ready to whirl and gallop away.

Strider looked back at her. She shivered the skin on her shoulders and lifted her head so that he could see the white rimming her eyes.

The scent scared her.

Strider stopped, lifting his own head. She could hear him taking short, quick breaths, sifting the air. And she knew the instant that the odd scent came to him.

He went completely still, listening, breathing deeply.

There was no breeze. It was impossible to tell which direction the scent had come from.

Esperanza turned her head slightly to see behind herself. There was no motion. Overhead the birds still sang. The frogs were still croaking in the pond.

His step careful, the muscles in his neck a tense ridge, Strider started forward.

Esperanza followed.

There was a strange arrangement of logs just beyond the cottonwoods. It was something like beavers' work, but much bigger, and there was no water around it. And the shape was all wrong; it was too tall, and it had straight-edged *corners*.

The horses approached slowly.

The logs had been cut, Esperanza saw, but this was a kind of beaver she knew nothing about. Instead of the chewed notches being scattered throughout a messy, mounded pile, they were all at the ends. And the logs had been piled in the oddest way—each one lay directly on top of the one below it, in strange, straight rows that joined at the notched corners.

This had nothing to do with beavers, Esperanza realized. What kind of beaver could drag logs this size? What beaver would stack them like this? And there was no scent of beavers here—only the strange smell that she had never encountered before in her life.

Strider edged forward, his muzzle extended. Esperanza watched, unable to make herself follow.

Strider touched the stacked logs, then backed away, curling his upper lip in order to smell the scent he had picked up. He shook his mane and glanced around. Esperanza could tell he was puzzled and uneasy, too. So he didn't recognize the scent either. That made her even more nervous.

They walked around the strange logged shape. There was an opening on one side. Esperanza looked at it. An entrance. So, this was a den of some kind. But a den for *what*?

Esperanza glanced behind herself again. There was no motion as far as she could see. She shivered her skin, nervous. Strider walked away from the log pile, and she hurried to catch up, afraid to be alone.

Behind the log pile was a pit, almost like a dust wallow. Esperanza edged toward it, unable to believe what she was seeing. It was full of burned wood and ashes!

How could a fire have been this small? When lightning started fires, it almost always spread. And there were no trees. Where was the tree the lightning had hit?

Esperanza saw Strider staring at the ashes, and she knew he was wondering the same things. She took a cautious step toward the pit and bent to sniff at it.

The fire had gone out a long, long time ago. Snow and rain had rinsed through the ashes many times. She pawed at them, and a clinking sound startled her into dancing backward.

Strider jumped when she did, and they stood stiffly, their heads up, their eyes wide.

Nothing happened.

The birds overhead were silent a moment, then they began singing again. Esperanza knew there was no real danger or they would have flown. She edged back toward the pit and lowered her head.

There was something shiny in the ashes. It had a strange odor, like everything else about this place. She touched it with her muzzle. It was cool, almost cold to touch. She wrinkled her upper lip to test the scent it had left on her skin.

It was like nothing she had ever scented before.

Strider joined her, lifting his head and wrinkling his lip, too.

Esperanza sniffed at it a second time and saw her image reflected in the silvery surface. It was like looking into still pond water, except that this image was distorted. Her muzzle looked as big as the moon and her ears looked tiny.

Esperanza snorted and stepped back. Nothing made sense here. Strange small fires that had burned without lightning, piles of logs that were so big a bear would have had trouble moving them—and piled up so straight they should have fallen, but hadn't. And what was the rounded silvery thing? What sort of animal had lived here?

Strider backed away from the pit, turning slowly. He tilted his head, staring at something on the ground, then started off. Esperanza followed, uneasy. Whatever he had seen, she would be happier leaving it alone.

Half hidden behind a second stand of cottonwoods, there was another strange, straight pile of logs—another enormous den—sticking up out of the ground and standing even taller than the first. It had a huge entrance. It was wide enough for two or three bears to enter, walking side by side.

Strider stood back from the opening, hesitating tensely, torn between caution and curiosity. Esperanza went to stand beside him. Together they inched forward, listening, scenting the air. There was no sound, no new scents. And the birds and frogs sang sleepily all around them.

At the entrance, Strider extended his neck, reaching out to look inside. Then he took a step. Trembling, Esperanza followed his example. She blinked in the darkness.

There was a scent here, as old as all the rest, that reminded her of deer, but was not deer. It was some kind of grass eater, she was sure. It had lived here. Its dung was a thick layer on the ground. How could there be an animal that grazed on these plains that she had never seen?

A dark shape lying on the ground caught her eye and she shied, bumping into Strider.

When they were sure it was not moving, was not

alive, they approached it. Esperanza stood transfixed. The thing was strange beyond imagining. No mushroom in the high forests, no wind-bent pine had ever had a stranger shape.

The thing was curved, almost like a horse's back, on one side, but on the other a knob stuck up at one end, a low ridge on the other.

Esperanza lowered her head to smell it. And she froze in fear. It smelled of horses. But the scent was mixed with the strange smell that clung to the log piles and with another, foul smell that made her shiver, something long dead—that had somehow not rotted back into the earth. She touched her muzzle to the thing and then recoiled. It felt like skin. But it had never been alive. Had it?

Esperanza shook her mane nervously. Whatever this thing was, it had been wet with horse sweat a hundred times or more.

But why? Had the horses been killed? Eaten?

Esperanza's nerves gave way, and she whirled, galloping out of the den's entrance, back through the cottonwoods and all the way down the long valley.

Strider was right behind her, staying close, his own breath steadier, but when Esperanza glanced at him, she saw that his eyes were rimmed in white. He was as frightened as she was.

This was not their homeland. It could never be. Whatever it was that had lived here might come back. And they did not want to be here on that terrible day.

Chapter Nine

*W*e galloped a long time. Once we were out of the strange creatures' valley, the country was brown and dry again, on every side. We traveled for days, grazing on nothing but prickly weeds and scrub brush. We kept hoping to find another good valley, but we didn't. What we found was of much less use to us. . . .

Late one morning, they topped a little rise and saw a group of antelope playing, springing across the land in their long, arcing leaps. As the graceful animals bounded away, Esperanza looked out over the brush country ahead of them. The mountains got bigger each day, but they still seemed far off.

There was very little shade in this dry country. The day before they had made do with a tall stand of hawthorns, easing themselves in among the spines, then easing back out when the sun began to fall westward and it had cooled off enough to travel again. Today, she saw no cottonwoods or hawthorns at all.

The summer gnats were hatching, and Esperanza was constantly flicking her ears and switching her tail to keep them off. Strider walked beside her, so that their tails swept across each other's backs.

Midday, they came upon a path. It smelled of deer and antelope and jackrabbits and wolves. With so many different animals using it, Esperanza knew instantly where it must lead: to water! But which way?

She stood quietly, in the still air. Strider lifted his own head and faced the opposite direction. There wasn't much breeze. Still, Esperanza smelled a faint scent of wet soil somewhere off to the north. She veered off the path.

As she walked, she flicked her ears, shooing the gnats that clouded around her head. Strider reached out to touch her shoulder and she slowed until they were walking side by side again. She rubbed her muzzle on Strider's shoulder to ease an itching gnat bite.

Then, without warning, the earth beneath her hooves simply gave way. Esperanza fell sideways, straining one foreleg as she crashed awkwardly on her side. Strider leaped clear, then the ground gave way beneath him. He stumbled, going down hard.

Esperanza struggled upright, then managed to stand again, wincing at a sharp pain in her right foreleg. Strider scrambled up after her, spinning in a tight circle to see what had attacked them, what had happened.

But there was nothing to see.

Esperanza extended her aching right foreleg, grunting a little with pain.

Strider reached to touch her neck, taking a single step toward her.

The ground gave away beneath him again, but this time he was ready for it and did not lose his balance. Esperanza stared at the uncertain ground before them.

There were small holes here and there in the soil. As she watched, a slim, furry animal popped up out of one of them, swiveled its head to look at her, then disappeared again. It made a squeaky whistling sound.

Esperanza looked at Strider. He shook his mane and took another cautious step. This time, the ground supported him. But on his next step it caved in again. Esperanza held still, the pain in her foreleg making her wary.

She looked down at the dirt where Strider stood fetlock-deep in crumbling soil. She could see a round opening, a little tunnel beneath the soil surface.

Another whistling call made Esperanza look up. Off to her left, another of the little creatures had emerged. She heard three or four responses to its call before it ducked back down. How many of them *were* there?

Esperanza took a careful step. The ground held

her weight. A second step was firm and steady as well. The third sent her jolting straight downward halfway up to her knees. Her right foreleg shot a pain up into her shoulder. Esperanza shook her mane, hard. She had seen gopher holes in the foothills, of course, but gophers didn't live in underground *herds* like this.

Strider began to pick his way forward. Esperanza followed, staying a little behind him so she could wait when he stumbled.

The burrows seemed endless. They struggled onward, their breath coming quick and fearful. How many horses had broken legs in these burrows? Esperanza wondered as they went on in their slow, hitching gait. How many had been fleeing wolves or hunger-bold coyotes and stumbled into this terrible place?

If they had been cantering ... Esperanza shivered the skin on her shoulders. If they had been cantering, one or both of them might be lying crippled.

Taking one careful step at a time, they made their way across the treacherous soil. Esperanza followed

Strider, stepping in his tracks where she could. Her right foreleg hurt, but she knew she had been lucky.

A sudden hissing sound near her right front hoof made her flinch. Strider jumped, lurching as the ground collapsed beneath him.

A tiny red-gold head peeked out of a ruined burrow. A slinky, shiny-coated animal sat up, its tiny paws tucked beneath its chin.

Esperanza blinked. This wasn't one of the tunnelers. This was something much worse. A weasel.

Strider turned around, ready to rear, to protect Esperanza, then he saw the little animal and stepped backward. Esperanza backed up a half step, awkwardly. Her leg hurt and she was afraid to trust the ground.

The weasel chose not to recognize their polite retreat. Instead of going back into its burrow, it came out. It stared straight at Esperanza, ignoring Strider completely. It advanced, its slender body moving in waves, like a snake crossing rough ground. Then, suddenly, it darted forward, its needle teeth bared.

Esperanza knew how fierce an angry weasel could be. She didn't want to fight this one, especially not on uncertain ground—and not with her foreleg already injured. She faced the enraged weasel, afraid that if she turned aside, it would rush in and tear at her legs.

Strider pranced forward, and for an instant the weasel looked at him instead of Esperanza. But the little animal knew which of these clumsy horses had nearly stepped on it. And that was the one that needed a lesson.

Esperanza backed up again, but the weasel only stiffened its front legs and whirled around threateningly. Strider jumped aside. An instant later, the air was full of a scent so strong, so terrible, that Esperanza's eyes stung.

She caught her breath, but it was too late. The awful, burning mist went down her throat, stinging and choking her. She coughed, stumbling backward.

The weasel ran and disappeared so quickly that Esperanza knew it had gone back underground. There had to be passages everywhere.

Her eyes streaming, Esperanza wheeled around, ignoring the pain in her foreleg. She wanted to run, to escape the horrible stench that burned her eyes and nostrils, but Strider came close, standing in her way. He would not let her gallop over this dangerous ground.

Once she had calmed down, Strider let her walk. He led the way, making sure she went slowly. A few hours later, with Esperanza limping, they found a little pond. Esperanza waded in, letting the cool water soak through her coat. Her knee was a little swollen now, and it ached in rhythm with her pulse.

Strider stood close beside her—but not too close. Esperanza didn't blame him. The weasel stink was terrible.

But as the sun went down, she noticed that even the mosquitoes stayed away from her. She heard an owl hooting as she fell asleep.

The next morning, Esperanza's leg had stiffened. Strider led the way. Esperanza followed, limping But as the sun rose in the sky, her leg limbered and they kept up almost their normal pace.

Coming over a rise, the horses came upon three does and their fawns. They looked up, mildly surprised, then the weasel scent reached them. They scrambled to get away from the smell, the long-legged fawns bounding along like leaves in a gusty wind.

Esperanza lowered her head. How long would the smell cling to her coat?

Come evening, they found a nice copse of trees—of a kind Esperanza had never seen before. They were tall and leafy and spread out almost as well as cottonwoods did. Strider settled a little farther from her than usual, and she noticed he had positioned himself upwind.

They were settling in to sleep when Esperanza heard a small, throaty little sound. She tensed, recognizing it. Strider did, too; she could tell by the long sighing sound as he exhaled.

The *chuk-chuk* sound got louder, and Esperanza stood still, as though she had no idea in the world *what* this new weasel was upset about. She knew, of course. It thought she was a rival—she *smelled* like a weasel, after all.

The little animal circled her, sniffing in a way that made its whiskers jump up and down. Esperanza stretched out her achy foreleg and rubbed her muzzle on it. Then she swished her tail and stared off at the sunset. It did no good at all.

The weasel came toward her, slinking, its mouth open to show its wicked little teeth. Esperanza backed up, amazed and furious.

What was wrong with this creature? Surely it could *see*—no matter what she smelled like—that she wasn't some oversized weasel invading its territory?

Esperanza stamped her sound foreleg. But instead of startling the weasel into moving away, she only managed to make it angry enough to advance. The snarling little animal darted toward her. Backing up a step at a time, Esperanza led the way as the weasel slowly chased her out from beneath the trees, and all the way down the hill.

Strider could only follow.

Esperanza was afraid to turn to flee, afraid to

take her eyes off the snarling, spitting weasel for an instant.

She lifted her head and shook her mane, then stamped a back hoof. But instead of noticing that she was tall, and had a mane and tail and hooves—that she was a *horse*—the weasel just kept coming.

Finally, Strider came forward, his teeth bared and his head low. The weasel whipped around and looked over its shoulder to take aim. Then it let fly a stream of its own scent.

Strider shook his head, snorting and blinking. Only then did the furious little animal walk away, headed back toward its den beneath the trees. Strider wheeled around and cantered off, and Esperanza followed.

That night they slept side by side again. There was no reason not to. They both smelled awful.

Chapter Ten

It took a long time for the wind to rinse the weasel-stink from our coats. We kept moving, crossing more brown plains, then we came into the foothills. The nights were cooler in the high country, but it was still summer. We often saw storm clouds rolling over our heads. They billowed on, piling up along the spine of the mountains, then rolling down the other side. The smell of rain convinced Strider to cross the mountains—rainy country usually meant there would be plenty of grass.

Esperanza switched her tail as she followed Strider along the edge of the sparse pine forest. It felt *wrong* to be ascending the mountains in the full, warm days of summer.

In their old homeland, the winter winds on the plains were murderous—and there was no grass at all. So the horses retreated to the mountain valleys in the fall and chewed willow shoots all winter. In spring, they walked back down to the plains when the grass began to grow.

But the foothills were beautiful, and there was enough grass to keep them strong. Esperanza loved waking next to Strider in the early dawn. Almost every morning was the same. He reached out to touch her gently, then stretched and shook his mane to wake up. Finally he inhaled deep drafts of the cool morning air, making sure no dangerous animals had come close in the night.

One morning they woke to a strange sound. Esperanza tensed, listening. It was a terrible noise, like nothing she had ever heard before.

Esperanza glanced at Strider. He seemed un-worried, relaxed. So she tried to calm herself as he began to walk. She followed a few steps behind him, passing through a stand of scattered pines. The red-orange pine needles crunched beneath their hooves, sending up sweet clouds of pine scent.

Esperanza was too nervous to enjoy the scent. The sound got louder as they went, and she tried hard to spot whatever was making it. She couldn't.

As the grating sound got louder, Esperanza hung back a little. What sort of animal rasped like that in its throat? Was it an animal? There was no wind—it couldn't just be branches scraping against each other.

They passed through a high meadow, then back into the shade of tall pines. Esperanza breathed in the familiar scent of deer mixed into the sharp sweet smell of the pine needles. She trotted to catch up with Strider. At that instant, the grating sound got even louder.

Esperanza touched Strider's shoulder. He glanced at her, then looked forward again.

There was no fear in his eyes, but Esperanza slowed a little anyway, hanging back again. Then she stopped and stared. Through the trees she could see a buck deer. But he looked different from any deer she had ever seen. It took her a moment to realize why. He was wearing his full, spreading summer antlers. And he was the one making the sound.

He was polishing his antlers against a tree trunk. He lunged forward, throwing his weight into the chore, his shoulder muscles in raised ridges under his sleek summer coat.

Esperanza caught her breath. Strider had known the sound, somehow. But she hadn't. She had seen shed antlers on the ground. She had seen the sweeping scars carved into the trunks of pine trees—all her life. She had discovered as a filly that both the fallen antlers and the trees had been covered with the musky smell of stag deer.

Esperanza had realized, more or less, that the antlers had once been part of the deer. But to see the stag close up like this, magnificent and strong, rubbing his antlers against the pine trunk, was a very different thing.

The deer suddenly saw them and leaped back from the tree as it turned to face them. Strider stopped and lowered his head a little, letting the deer know that they meant no harm.

Esperanza followed his example, hoping the stag would understand.

The stag stared at them a moment, blinking. Esperanza was sure it felt foolish. It should. If two horses could simply walk up to it, wolves certainly could, as long as they were careful to stay upwind.

The stag suddenly shook its head, and Esperanza was amazed that it could manage the weight of its antlers so well. They looked so heavy, so awkward, like small trees growing sideways from its skull.

The stag snorted. For the first time, Esperanza heard tiny rustles in the trees around them. The stag was not alone. As the stag moved off, she watched, fascinated, as it somehow made its way through the pine branches without getting stuck.

Behind it came three graceful does, their fawns at their sides. Their cloven hooves bruised the reddish pine needles on the ground, sending up clouds of pine scent.

Strider walked close to the scarred tree trunk

and sniffed at it. Esperanza joined him. The stag had left a strong marking scent on the bark. That meant he wanted other stags to know he had been here—that this was his homeland.

Esperanza sighed as they went on. She could see narrow, barely visible trails crisscrossing the mountainside. The scent on the bushes and in the soil was unmistakable. These were deer trails.

Esperanza's heart sank. These mountains might not be a good place for them to winter. It would be hard to find willow in the valleys, since so many deer lived here as well.

They kept moving. Following a deep gorge with a rushing river at its bottom, they emerged into a kind of country Esperanza had never seen before.

There were still pine tress, as in the mountains she had known all her life. But the creek bottoms here were choked with flowers and plants. There were so many kinds that their scents seemed to crowd the very air.

Strider seemed as baffled by it as she was. He stopped many times a day to carefully sniff at each new plant, rippling his upper lip across the leaves, then curling it upward to take in the scents he had just gathered.

Esperanza breathed in the odors of the new plants, too. None smelled like the poisonous plants she had grown up around, but she was still cautious about eating them.

Strider was careful, too, she noticed. He ate only the kinds of plants that had been grazed upon by some other animal. Esperanza followed his example. It was almost certainly safe. Surely the deer and rabbits that lived here knew what was good to eat.

As they descended the far side of the mountain range, they walked, step-by-step, back into the heat of summer. The grass grew thicker and tougher and the delicate plants of the mountains disappeared.

One morning at sunrise, Esperanza looked out at the plains and she began to hope again. There was so much room here. Surely they would be able to find a place to begin a new herd, a place where they could live safely.

She stared at the horizon as the sun came up

over the mountains behind her. A glimmer of silver at the very edge of the horizon caught her attention. Strider lifted his head and she knew that he had seen it, too.

A river!

Together, they started off.

They walked side by side, their shoulders brushing. After a few minutes Strider broke into a trot, then a gallop.

Esperanza kept up, galloping when he did.

It became a race.

Esperanza flattened out, running hard, determined not to let Strider win. He leaped a clump of sage, then a second later they rose together, jumping a deep erosion ditch.

Esperanza nipped at his shoulder and he swerved, then came back, pretending to nip back at her. Esperanza dodged away, and the race turned into a game of bucking and rearing. They played like colts until they were winded. Then, still walking close, they set off again.

Chapter Eleven

I really thought we had found our home that morning. All through the day, I felt like galloping again. We did not graze until evening, and then we found the grass sparse. The next morning we awoke and realized that even though these plains had looked like a perfect new home from a distance, there was no grass left. Something had grazed it flat. The animals had left behind their odd scent—it was thick with musk and dust.

By the second day, Esperanza was hungry. She was also uneasy. There were big thunderstorms to the north. They could hear the rumbling in the dark, distant clouds. The wind brought them the scent of heavy rain. That night they slept in the open.

The next morning, Esperanza looked back at the mountains they had crossed. The grass between where she stood now and the foothills was poor and thin and grazed nearly to the ground by some mysterious beasts that had left an unfamiliar scent everywhere.

Esperanza saw Strider looking at her. She faced the mountains and took a single step to show him what she was thinking. Maybe they should go back into the foothills in spite of all the deer.

Strider moved to stand in front of her. He nuzzled her neck, and she closed her eyes for a moment. Strider was hungry, too, she was sure. It had been nearly impossible to find any grass. But it was very clear that he didn't want to retrace their steps.

Esperanza looked toward the mountains again, then turned to face in the direction of the river. They would find grass soon. They would have to.

Esperanza led off, walking toward the glittering shine that marked the course of the river. If they traveled steadily, they would probably reach it the following day. She could see clumps of trees growing beside it.

Esperanza hoped, starting off, that the grazing would be better that day. But it wasn't. It was terrible. The grass had been sparse to begin with, and the dusty-scent animals had simply eaten it down to the ground. She plodded along, losing heart again, her head low and her ears tilted backward.

Strider pretended to nip at her. He arched his neck and trotted in a circle around her.

Esperanza ignored him. She was tired of traveling and tired of being hungry.

Strider whinnied suddenly. Esperanza turned as he trotted away from her, then stopped and looked back. He shook his mane and pawed at the ground.

Esperanza went to look. For some reason a patch of tall grass had survived the grazing of the dust-scented animals. She eagerly tore off a mouthful of the grass. Then she looked at Strider.

He was not eating. He stood straight, alert for danger, his head up and his ears moving from side to side.

Esperanza nickered at him. He took one mouthful of grass, then stepped back again.

His meaning was clear. He would eat a little. But he wanted Esperanza to eat, to restore her strength and her spirits. Grateful, she lowered her head and began to graze.

That night, as Strider and Esperanza slept in the open again, the clouds rolled southward. They woke to a gray sky and the smell of rain. Low rumblings of thunder made Esperanza shiver, even though it had not yet begun to storm.

Strider stretched and switched his tail irritably.

Esperanza understood him perfectly.

It was going to be cold and rainy and they had not had enough to eat in days.

Esperanza touched him with her muzzle to thank him again for letting her eat her fill the day before. Now it was her turn to be brave. She started off—heading toward the river.

Strider trotted to catch up, then walked beside her.

As they went, the rumbling of the thunder got louder and there were distant flashes of lightning. By noon, the sky was dark gray and the flashes of lightning lit the earth, then crashed into thunder that shook the ground. Even so, it took a long time for the rain to start. Once it did, it rained hard.

The hissing of the raindrops as they fell muted even the shuddering roar of the thunder. Lightning flashed again, then again. Esperanza and Strider finally gave up and stopped. They were not going to find shelter, and it was miserable trying to walk against the heavy rain. They moved close together and lowered their heads, prepared to wait out the storm.

The next bolt of lightning hit the ground with a violent, deafening crack. It was so loud, so close, that Esperanza cringed. The thunder that followed it slammed into her ears, painful and scary—and it seemed to go on far too long.

Esperanza lifted her head, blinking as the rain

ran into her eyes. She looked to the west and saw a dark storm rolling along the ground. She blinked again.

Then she turned, instinctively, to face the dark mass, to see what the danger was. She caught her breath and stood staring. Strider had felt her move and lifted his own head to look. An instant later, he was pushing Esperanza along, whinnying frantically at her, leaping into a canter.

Esperanza rose into a gallop beside Strider. She glanced back, and saw something that made no sense. There was an unbroken wall of dark brown coming straight toward them.

Strider whinnied at her again, and she lowered her head to gallop faster. The thunder was still rumbling, even though the lightning had stopped flashing. That made no sense, Esperanza knew, but ...

She glanced behind them again and whinnied in fear.

The brown storm was animals. Woolly, heavy animals as massive as bears, with a strong, dusty smell. Esperanza blinked. Now she understood the grass shortage. Many of them had short, curved horns on their dark-wooled heads. She remembered these strong, heavy animals. She had seen them once before, when she had been a long-legged filly hiding behind her mother as they passed. *Buffalo.* The huge herd seemed to stretch out the length of the horizon, and they were all running flat out.

Strider squealed and stretched out, covering the ground in desperate leaps. Esperanza lunged into a headlong gallop that matched Strider's speed, and the two of them pounded toward the river.

The thunderous rumbling of the hooves behind them went on and swelled. It was coming closer.

Strider angled their course a little and Esperanza risked another glance backward. She could see the animals more clearly now. They were running close together, their wooled shoulders touching, their mouths open as they gasped for breath.

Strider squealed and Esperanza tried to keep up as he angled their course a second time. Esperanza knew what he was trying to do.

If they could just find the end of the huge herd, they could get out of the way.

Esperanza glanced away from the animals and

realized that she and Strider would never make it. The river was curving toward them. The banks were getting higher and steeper. They were going to run out of room.

Strider saw the danger at the same instant, and he whinnied, driving himself forward. His desperation made Esperanza's hooves fly. Together they charged ahead, frantic to escape. But the distance between them and the river was diminishing with every stride.

Strider veered suddenly, whinnying desperately at Esperanza. Sure she was about to die beneath thousands of hooves, she followed him without question, pounding at breakneck speed, straight at the high banks of the river.

And when he jumped into thin air, she was right behind him.

The muddy, rough water was deep and cool and Esperanza plunged beneath it, paddling wildly with all four legs. For a terrifying moment she could not tell which way was up, the water seemed to enclose her entirely, holding her down. Then she exploded back into the air and dragged in a long breath.

For an instant she thought she was alone in the water, that Strider had not lived through the leap. Then she saw him behind her, struggling to turn in the current. She knew he was looking for her.

Throwing her head high, she whinnied, and he thrashed in a half circle to face her. He whinnied back. Esperanza glanced wildly at the banks. There were no buffalo in sight. They had managed to stop—or had veered off. She whinnied once more, then wrenched back around in the water, trying to keep her head above the current.

The river kept them apart for a long time. Esperanza tried to make her way to the bank, but it was impossible. The deep channel she was in was running so swiftly that it was all she could do to keep her head above the surface.

The river took another bend, and Esperanza was washed in a long curve, the riverbank sliding past at a dizzying speed. Her back hoof struck something solid, then glanced off.

Rocks?

Esperanza twisted around to look back at Strider. He was still fighting the current, his mane flying, his eyes full of fury and fear.

Esperanza whinnied at him and he answered her.

She faced into the current again, her mouth and nostrils full of the muddy water. She squeezed her eyes shut to clear her vision and stared ahead.

There.

The banks spread out up ahead, and for a short distance, the river widened. The water would run slower there. Just beyond that, the river ran between two steep bluffs. She could hear the low roar of rough water beyond the bluffs. Esperanza called to Strider, then began swimming hard.

Driving her weary legs against the relentless current, Esperanza struggled desperately. She knew they had to make it to the bank when the current slowed.

Forcing herself not to look up—or downstream—she called out to Strider again and again as she forced herself to keep swimming. Her breath came in sobs and her muscles cramped. Esperanza kept swimming; she knew she had no choice.

Finally, her back hoof struck something hard again. Then one of her forehooves nicked a solid surface. The bottom! The water was shallow enough to stand. She steadied herself, wrenching around to see if Strider had made it.

He was still flailing in the deep water and she turned to whinny at him, pleading with him not to give up. When he finally staggered into the shallows, they simply stood close together, heaving in long breaths, too weak to climb the bank.

Chapter Twelve

We finally waded out of the river together, exhausted. We made our way to a stand of cottonwoods and stayed in their shelter the rest of the day, dozing, trying to stay warm as the rain poured down around us. But the next morning, when the day dawned clear and bright, we were so hungry we knew we had to travel.

Esperanza led off, following no particular path. Strider walked with her. Both of them were scanning the horizon, scenting the air, their nostrils flared for the odd scent of buffalo, for any sign of wolves or any other danger that might mean they would have to gallop away from this beautiful valley. But no dangerous scents came to them.

Esperanza saw the stand of grass first. It was so green and so tall that for a moment she thought she must be mistaken. Then she heard Strider pull in a quick, happy breath, and she knew she wasn't imagining anything.

They trotted side by side, then stopped in unison, lowering their heads to eat. The sun climbed high in the morning sky before either one of them stopped chewing.

When they did lift their heads, full for the first time in days, Esperanza reached out to touch Strider's muzzle with her own.

Together they walked down the long slope to the river that ran down the center of the valley. It was deep in places, but they found a shallow ford and crossed. The water was sweet and clear and they drank deep before they waded out.

There was grass on the far side of the river, too,

and stands of cottonwood and willow. They found a fine stand of trees growing along the foot of a bluff.

It rained in the afternoon. Esperanza watched the clouds. They floated overhead, then piled up against the mountains at the far end of the valley. Held back by the high range, they spilled their rain. It was no accident that this valley was greener than the ones she had grown up in.

They slept at the base of the bluff that night. The next morning, they woke in the dusk just before dawn. Strider led the way into the deep grass, walking with his head high. His step was light and happy, and Esperanza knew why.

This valley was perfect.

Esperanza nudged him. When he tossed his head, startled, she nudged him again. Then she whirled and galloped away in the soft predawn light. Strider chased her.

They played for a long time, crisscrossing the valley, racing around the plum thickets and willow stands. They found a fallen log and jumped it side-by-side, then galloped in a long circle so that they could do it a second time.

The air was warming up fast and sleepy birds were beginning to waken as they raced along a creek, splashing through the water to cross it.

When they finally slowed Esperanza heard a high, whistling cry and looked up to see two tiny specks of gold brown against the dawn-pink sky.

It was a pair of eagles, lifelong mates, flying in wide overlapping spirals. They called to each other again, and their cries carried from one end of the valley to the other.

Esperanza stood close to Strider.

It had been hard—and she had almost given up— but they had found a perfect place at last. This wide valley would shelter them. Its river would give them water, the grass would feed them well.

Esperanza stared out at the deep green grass and imagined a herd of horses grazing there, healthy and strong, the foals leaping in circles, racing and playing.

Strider shook his mane and moved closer. They stood quietly together, their shoulders touching as they watched the sun rise on their new homeland.